Hans Christian Andersen

FAVORITE FAIRY TALES

Illustrated by Paul Durand

Translation courtesy of The Hamlyn Publishing Group Limited

GOLDEN PRESS • NEW YORK
® Western Publishing Company, Inc.
Racine, Wisconsin

Contents

The Shepherdess
and the Chimney Sweep

Have you ever seen an old-fashioned oak cabinet, black with age and covered, every inch of it, with carved foliage and curious figures? Just such a cabinet, an heirloom, once the property of its present owner's great-grandmother, stood in a parlor. It was covered from top to bottom with carved roses and tulips, and little stags' heads with long branching antlers peered forth from the curious scrolls and foliage surrounding them. In the middle of the cabinet was carved the full-length figure of a man, who seemed to be perpetually grinning, perhaps at himself, for in truth he was a most ridiculous figure. He had crooked legs like a goat, small horns on his forehead, and a long beard. The children of the house used to call him Field-Marshal-Major-General-Corporal-Sergeant Billy-goat's Legs. This was a long, hard name, and not many figures, in wood or stone, could boast of such a title. There he stood, his eyes always fixed upon the table under the mirror, for on this table stood a pretty little porcelain shepherdess, wearing a red rose, with her gown gathered gracefully round her. Her shoes and hat were gilt, her

hand held a crook; she was a most charming figure. Close by her stood a little chimney sweep as black as coal, and made, like the shepherdess, of porcelain. He was as clean and neat as any other china figure. Indeed, the manufacturer might just as well have made a prince of him as a chimney sweep, for though elsewhere black as coal, his face was as fresh and rosy as a girl's, which was certainly a mistake—it ought to have been black. With his ladder in his hand, he kept his place close by the little shepherdess. They had been put side by side from the first, had always remained on

the same spot, and so had plighted their troth to each other. They suited each other well, for they were both young, both of the same kind of china, and both alike, fragile and delicate.

Near them stood another figure three times as large as they were, and also made of porcelain. He was an old Chinese mandarin who could nod his head, and he declared that he was grandfather of the little shepherdess. He could not prove this, but he

insisted that he had authority over her, and so, when Field-Marshal-Major-General-Corporal-Sergeant Billy-goat's Legs made proposals to the little shepherdess, he nodded his head in token of his consent.

"Now you will have a husband," said the old mandarin to her, "who, I verily believe, is made of mahogany. You will be the wife of a Field-Marshal-Major-General-Corporal-Sergeant, of a man who has a whole cabinet full of silver plate, besides a store of no one knows what in the secret drawers."

"I will not go into that dismal cabinet," said the little shepherdess. "I have heard that he has eleven china wives already imprisoned there."

"Then you shall be the twelfth, and you will be in good company," said the mandarin. "This very night, as soon as you hear a noise in the old cabinet, you shall be married, as sure as I am a mandarin," and then he nodded his head and fell asleep.

But the little shepherdess wept, and turned to her betrothed, the china chimney sweep.

"I believe I must beg you," said she, "to go out with me into the wide world, for we cannot stay here."

"I will do everything you wish," said the little chimney sweep. "Let us go at once. I think I can support you by my profession."

"If we could only get safely off the table!" sighed she. "I shall never be happy till we are really out in the world."

Then he comforted her, and showed her how to set her little foot on the carved edges and gilded foliage twining round the leg of the table. He helped her with his little ladder, and at last they reached the floor. But when they turned to look at the old cabinet, they saw that it was all astir: the carved stags were putting their little heads farther out, raising their antlers and moving

their throats, while Field-Marshal-Major-General-Corporal-Sergeant Billy-goat's Legs was jumping up and down and shouting to the old Chinese mandarin, "Look, they are running away! They are running away!" The runaways were dreadfully frightened and jumped into an open drawer under the windowsill.

In this drawer there were three or four packs of cards, none of them complete, and also a little puppet theater which had

been set up as neatly as it could be. A play was then going on, and all the queens, whether diamonds, hearts, clubs, or spades, sat in the front row fanning themselves with the flowers they held in their hands, while behind them stood the knaves, showing that they had each two heads, one above and one below, as most cards have. The play was about two persons who were in love, but could not marry, and the shepherdess wept over it, for it was just like her own story.

"I cannot bear this!" said she. "Let us leave the drawer." But when they again got to the floor, on looking up at the table they saw that the old Chinese mandarin was awake, and that his whole body was shaking to and fro with rage.

"Oh, the old mandarin is coming!" cried the little shepherdess, and down she fell on her knees in the greatest distress.

"A thought has struck me," said the chimney sweep. "Let us creep into the large potpourri vase that stands in the corner;

there we can rest upon roses and lavender, and throw salt in his eyes if he comes near us."

"That will not do at all," said she, "for many years ago the mandarin was betrothed to the potpourri vase, and there is always a kindly feeling between people who have been so intimate as that. No, there is no help for us; we must wander forth together into the wide world!"

"Have you indeed the courage to go with me into the wide world?" asked the chimney sweep. "Have you thought how large it is, and that we may never return?"

"I have," replied she.

The chimney sweep looked fixedly at her, and when he saw that she was firm, he said, "My path leads through the chimney. Have you indeed the courage to creep with me through the stove and up the pipe? I know the way well! We shall climb up so high that they cannot come near us, and at the top there is a hole that leads into the wide world."

He led her to the door of the stove.

"How black it looks!" sighed she, but she went on with him, through the stove and up the pipe, where it was dark, pitch dark.

"Now we are in the chimney," said he, "and look, what a lovely star shines over us."

And it really was a star, shining right down upon them, as if to show them the way. So they climbed and crawled; it was a fearful path, so dreadfully steep and seemingly endless, but the little sweep lifted her and held her, and showed her the best places to plant her tiny porcelain feet on, till at last they reached the edge of the chimney. There they sat down to rest, for they were very tired.

The sky with all its stars was above them, and the town with all its roofs lay beneath them. They could see all round them far out into the wide world. The poor little shepherdess had never dreamed of anything like this; she leaned her little head on the chimney sweep's arm, and wept so bitterly that the gilding broke off from her waistband.

"This is too much!" she cried. "The world is all too large! Oh that I were once more upon the little table under the mirror! I shall never be happy till I am there again. I have followed you

into the wide world; surely if you love me you can follow me home again."

The chimney sweep talked sensibly to her, reminding her of the old mandarin and Field-Marshal-Major-General-Corporal-Sergeant Billy-goat's Legs. But she wept so bitterly, and kissed her little chimney sweep so fondly, that at last he could not but yield to her request, foolish as it was.

So with great trouble they crawled down the chimney, crept through the pipe and into the dark stove. They lurked for a little

behind the door, listening, before they would venture to return
to the room. Everything was quite still. They peeped out. Alas!
on the floor lay the old mandarin. In trying to follow the runaways, he had jumped down from the table and had broken into
three pieces. His head lay shaking in a corner. The Field-Marshal-
Major-General-Corporal-Sergeant Billy-goat's Legs stood where
he had always stood, thinking over what had happened.

"Oh, how shocking!" exclaimed the little shepherdess. "My old
grandfather is broken into pieces, and it is all our fault! I shall
never get over it!" and she wrung her little hands.

"He can be put together again," said the chimney sweep. "He

can very easily be put together; only don't be so impatient! If they glue his back together and put a strong rivet in his neck, then he will be as good as new and will be able to say plenty of unpleasant things to us."

"Do you really think so?" asked she. And then they climbed up the table to the place where they had stood before.

"Well, we're not much farther on," said the chimney sweep. "We might have spared ourselves all the trouble."

"If we could only have old grandfather put together!" said the shepherdess. "Will it cost very much?"

He was put together. The family had his back glued and his neck riveted. He was as good as new, but could no longer nod his head.

"We have certainly grown very proud since we were broken into pieces," said Field-Marshal-Major-General--Corporal-Sergeant Billy-goat's Legs, "but I must say, for my part, I do not see that there is anything to be proud of. Am I to have her or am I not? Just answer me that!"

The chimney sweep and the little shepherdess looked imploringly at the old mandarin; they were so afraid lest he should nod. But nod he could not, and it was disagreeable to him to have to tell a stranger that he had a rivet in his neck. So the young porcelain people were left together, and they blessed the grandfather's rivet, and loved each other till they broke into pieces.

The Little Match Girl

How cold it was! It had been snowing all day—and was still snowing as a little girl made her way along the dark narrow street. Already her hands and her bare feet were blue with cold.

It is true she had been wearing slippers when she left home, but they were her mother's slippers and were much too big for her. She had lost one as she ran across the road between two carriages, and the other had just dropped off and had been snatched by a boy as ragged as herself.

The girl clutched a bundle of matches in her small thin hands and the cruel wind tore at her patched skirt and stung her pale cheeks. Hour after hour she had tramped the snow-covered streets, hoping that some kind passerby would take her matches. But it was the last day of the Old Year and those who found themselves in the street were in too much of a hurry to get home

to their big dinners and warm fires to think about buying matches.

"I dare not return," the little girl thought miserably. "What would my father say if I had to tell him I had not sold a single bundle?"

In her mind's eye she could see the poverty stricken attic she had to call home—with the cracks in the wall stuffed with straw and rags to keep out the biting wind. "No, far better to stay outside, even when all the lights of the shops go out, and the streets are empty of people," she decided.

At the end of a row of shops, two gray-stoned houses stood close together. It was here between the houses that the match girl found a place to sit. How she shivered as she crouched low, trying to protect herself from the falling snow.

If only she dared to light one of the matches and warm her frozen fingers! At last, she took out a match and struck it against the wall . . . and, oh, how brightly it glowed in the darkness! The warm, pure flame was like a little candle when she covered it with her hand. For a moment, it seemed to the match girl that she was seated in front of a roaring fire in a beautiful room filled with ornaments. The fire was so cheerful and inviting that she stretched out her feet to warm them as well as her hands. Alas, the match burned itself out, and the vision vanished.

When the girl struck her second match, the light fell on the wall and there—instead of a cold gray wall—was a room, in the center of which stood a table covered with a white tablecloth and dainty china. A fat roast goose, stuffed with prunes and apples, sat on a silver serving dish, and oh, how good it smelled! There was so much food on the table that the little girl scarcely knew where to begin. Then, all of a sudden, the goose rolled off the dish and fell almost at her feet. But as she stretched out her hand, the match burned itself out, and there was nothing to touch but the solid gray wall.

Presently, the match girl struck a third match against the wall. Immediately, she found herself under a magnificent Christmas tree; it was taller and even more beautiful than the one she had seen last year in a shop window. Hundreds of candles twinkled on the green branches, and the spirit of Christmas itself seemed to shine out from the tree. Smiling in delight, the child reached towards the candles—but they suddenly began to rise. As the match went out, the Christmas tree disappeared, and the little girl saw that the Christmas candles, which were now high above her head, were really stars! One of the stars fell, leaving a bright trail across the heavens. And the little girl remembered how once her grandmother, the only person who had truly loved her, had talked about heaven before she died.

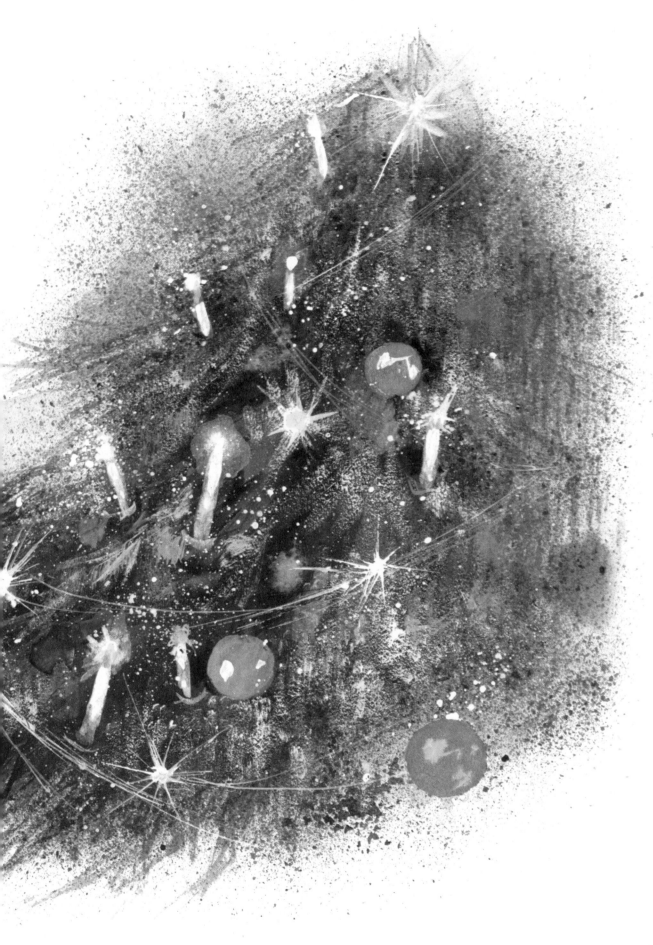

"How wonderful it would be to see my grandmother again," she thought as she struck her fourth match. The match blazed into life and there, caught in its dazzling flame, was her beloved grandmother, as sweet and radiant as she had once been in real life.

"Don't leave me, Grandmother," whispered the little girl. "I know that you will as soon as this match burns out. Please don't leave me. Stay with me, stay with me!" And she began to light one match after another in frantic haste. The matches gave off a light so dazzling that it was as if the sun were shining. Never had her grandmother looked so beautiful! Then the little girl

struck her very last match and her grandmother opened her arms and clasped the child to herself.

The match spluttered and died, dropping from the cold, lifeless hands of the match girl. She was found in the morning—the first day of the New Year.

"Poor child," said one of the women in the small crowd that had gathered. "She must have frozen to death!"

"Yet she looks happy," whispered her friend. "She looks as if she had seen something wonderful before she died!"

The Princess and the Pea

There was once a Prince who wished to marry a Princess; but she had to be a real Princess. He traveled all over the world in hopes of finding one, but there was always something wrong. Princesses he found in plenty, but he could not tell if they were real Princesses, for if not one thing, then another, seemed to him not quite right about them. At last he went back to his palace very downcast, because he wished so much to have a real Princess for his wife, and he had not been able to find one.

One evening a fearful storm arose. It thundered and lightninged, and the rain came down in torrents. Besides, it was as

dark as pitch. All at once there was a violent knocking at the door, and the old King, the Prince's father, went out himself to open it.

It was a Princess who was standing outside. What with the rain and the wind, she was in a sad state; the water trickled from her hair, and her clothes clung to her body. She said she was a real Princess.

"Ah, we shall soon see about that!" thought the old Queen mother. She gave no hint whatever of what she was going to do but went quietly into the bedroom, took all the bed clothes off the bed, and put a little pea on the bedstead. Then she laid twenty mattresses one upon another over the pea, and put twenty thick quilts over the mattresses.

Upon this bed the Princess was to pass the night.

The next morning she was asked how she had slept. "Oh, very badly indeed!" she replied. "I have scarcely closed my eyes the whole night through. I do not know what was in my bed, but I had something hard under me and am black-and-blue all over. It hurt me so much!"

Now it was plain that this must be a real Princess, since she had been able to feel the little pea through the twenty mattresses and twenty thick quilts. None but a real Princess could have had such a delicate sense of feeling.

So the Prince made her his wife, being now convinced that he had found a real Princess. The pea was, however, put into the royal museum, where it is still to be seen, if it has not been stolen.

The Ugly Duckling

How beautiful it was in the country! It was summer time; the wheat was yellow, the oats were green, the hay was stacked up in the meadows, and the stork strutted about on his long red legs, chatting in Egyptian, the language he had learned from his mother. The fields and meadows were skirted by thick woods, and in the midst of the woods lay a deep lake. Yes, it was indeed beautiful in the country! The sunshine fell warmly on an old country house, surrounded by deep canals, and from the walls down to the water's edge there grew large burdock leaves, so high that children could stand upright among them without being

seen. This place was as wild and lonely as the thickest part of the wood, and because of this a duck had chosen to make her nest there. She was sitting on her eggs, but the pleasure she had felt at first was now almost gone, because she had been there so long and had so few visitors, for the other ducks preferred swimming about in the canals to climbing up the slippery banks and sitting gossiping with her.

At last the eggs began to crack, and one little head after another appeared. "Quack, quack!" said the duck, and all got up as well as they could, and peeped about from under the green leaves.

"How large the world is!" said the little ones.

"Do you think this is the whole of the world?" said the mother. "It stretches far away beyond the other side of the garden down to the pastor's field, but I have never been there. Are you all here?" And then she got up. "No, the largest egg is still here. How long, I wonder, will this last? I am so weary of it!" And then she sat down again.

"Well! and how are you getting on?" asked an old duck, who had come to pay her a visit.

"This one egg keeps me so long," said the mother. "It will not break; but you should see the others! They are the prettiest little ducklings I have seen in all my days."

"Depend upon it," said the old duck, "it is a turkey's egg. I was cheated in the same way once myself, and I had such trouble with the young ones. They were so afraid of the water that I could not get them to go near it. I called and scolded, but it was

of no use. But let me see the egg. Ah, yes! to be sure, that is a turkey's egg. Leave it, and teach the other little ones to swim."

"I will sit on it a little longer," said the duck. "I have been sitting so long, that a day or two will not matter much."

"It is no business of mine," said the old duck, and away she waddled.

The great egg burst at last. "Peep, peep!" said the little one, and out it tumbled. But oh! how large and ugly it was! The duck looked at it. "That is a great, strong creature," said she. "None of the others are at all like it. Can it be a young turkey cock? Well, we shall soon find out. Into the water it must go, though I shall have to push it in myself."

The next day there was delightful weather, and the sun was shining warmly upon all the green leaves when mother duck with her family went down to the canal. Splash! she went into the

water. "Quack, quack!" cried she, and one duckling after another jumped in. The water closed over their heads, but all came up again and swam quite easily. All were there; even the ugly gray one was swimming about with the rest.

"No, it is not a turkey," said the mother duck. "See how prettily it moves its legs, how upright it holds itself. It is my own child, and it is really very pretty when one looks more closely at it. Quack! quack! now come with me, I will take you into the world; but keep close to me, or someone may tread on you. And beware of the cat."

When they came into the duck yard, two families were quarreling about the head of an eel, which in the end was carried off by the cat.

"See, my children, that is the way of the world," said the mother duck, whetting her beak, for she too was fond of roasted eels. "Now use your legs," said she, "keep together, and bow to the old duck you see yonder. She is the noblest born of them all, and is of Spanish blood, which accounts for her dignified appearance and manners. And look, she has a red rag on her leg; that is considered a special mark of distinction and is the greatest honor a duck can have."

The other ducks who were in the yard looked at them and said aloud, "Only see! now we have another brood, as if there were not enough of us already. And fie! how ugly that one is; we will not endure it." And immediately one of the ducks flew at him and bit him on the neck.

"Leave him alone," said the mother. "He is doing no one any harm."

"Yes, but he is so large, and so ungainly."

"Those are fine children that our good mother has," said the old duck with the red rag on her leg. "All are pretty except that one, who certainly is not at all well favored. I wish his mother could improve him a little."

"Certainly he is not handsome," said the mother, "but he is a very good child, and swims as well as the others, indeed rather better. I think in time he will grow like the others and perhaps will look smaller." And she stroked the duckling's neck and smoothed his ruffled feathers. "Besides," added she, "he is a drake; I think he will be very strong, so he will fight his way through."

"The other ducks are very pretty," said the old duck. "Pray make yourselves at home, and if you find an eel's head you can bring it to me."

And accordingly they made themselves at home.

But the poor duckling, who had come last out of his eggshell and who was so ugly, was bitten, pecked, and teased by both ducks and hens. And the turkey cock, who had come into the world with spurs on and therefore fancied he was an emperor, puffed himself up like a ship in full sail and marched up to the duckling quite red with passion. The poor thing scarcely knew what to do; he was quite distressed because he was so ugly.

So passed the first day, and afterwards matters grew worse and worse. Even his brothers and sisters behaved unkindly, and were constantly saying, "May the cat take you, you ugly thing!" while his mother said she wished he had never been born. The ducks bit him, the hens pecked him, and the girl who fed poultry kicked him. He ran through the hedge, and the little birds in the bushes were frightened and flew away. "That is because I am so ugly," thought the duckling, and ran on. At last he came to a wide moor, where some wild ducks lived. There he lay the whole night, feeling very tired and sorrowful. In the morning the wild ducks flew up, and then they saw their new companion. "Pray

who are you?" asked they, and the duckling greeted them as politely as possible.

"You are really very ugly," said the wild ducks; "but that does not matter to us if you do not wish to marry into our family."

Poor thing! he had never thought of marrying. He only wished to lie among the reeds and drink the water of the moor. There

he stayed for two whole days. On the third day there came two
wild geese, or rather goslings, for they had not long been out of
their eggshells, which accounts for their impertinence.

"Hark ye," said they, "you are so ugly that we like you very well.
Will you go with us and become a bird of passage? On another
moor, not far from this, are some dear, sweet, wild geese, as

lovely creatures as have ever said 'hiss, hiss.' It is a chance for you to get a wife; you may be lucky, ugly as you are."

Bang! a gun went off, and both goslings lay dead among the reeds. Bang! another gun went off, and whole flocks of wild geese flew up from the rushes. Again and again the same alarming noise was heard.

There was a great shooting party. The sportsmen lay in ambush all around; some were even sitting in the trees, whose huge branches overshadowed the rushes. The dogs splashed about in the mud, bending the reeds and rushes in all directions. How frightened the poor little duck was! He turned his head away, thinking to hide it under his wing, and at the same moment a fierce-looking dog passed close to him, his tongue hanging out of his mouth, his eyes sparkling fearfully. His jaws were wide open. He thrust his nose close to the duckling, showing his sharp, white teeth, and then—splash, splash! he was gone—gone without hurting him.

"Well! let me be thankful," sighed the duckling. "I am so ugly that even a dog will not bite me."

And so he lay still though the shooting continued among the reeds. The noise did not cease till late in the day, and even then the poor little thing dared not stir. He waited several hours before he looked round him, and then hastened away from the moor as fast as he could. He ran over fields and meadows, though the wind was so high that he could hardly go against it.

Towards evening he reached a wretched little hut, so wretched that it knew not on which side to fall and therefore remained standing. He noticed that the door had lost one of its hinges, and hung so much awry that there was a space between it and the wall wide enough to let him through. So, as the storm was becoming worse and worse, he crept into the room.

In this room lived an old woman, with her tom cat and her hen. The cat, whom she called her little son, knew how to arch his back and purr. He could even throw out sparks when his fur was stroked the wrong way. The hen had very short legs and was therefore called Chickie Shortlegs; she laid very good eggs, and the old woman loved her as her own child.

The next morning the cat began to mew and the hen to cackle when they saw the new guest.

"What is the matter?" asked the old woman, looking round. Her eyes were not good, so she took the duckling to be a fat duck who had lost her way. "This is a capital catch," said she. "I shall now have duck's eggs, if it is not a drake. We must wait and see." So the duckling was kept on trial for three weeks, but no eggs made their appearance.

Now the cat was the master of the house, and the hen was the mistress, and they used to always say, "We and the world," for

they imagined themselves to be not only one half of the world, but also by far the better half. The duckling thought it was possible to be of a different opinion, but that the hen would not allow.

"Can you lay eggs?" asked she.

"No."

"Well, then, hold your tongue."

And the cat said, "Can you curve your back? Can you purr?"

"No."

"Well, then you should have no opinion at all when sensible people are speaking."

So the duckling sat in a corner feeling very much dispirited till the fresh air and bright sunshine came into the room through the open door, and these gave him such a strong desire to swim that he could not help telling the hen.

"What ails you?" said the hen. "You have nothing to do and therefore brood over these fancies; either lay eggs, or purr, then you will forget them."

"But it is so delicious to swim," said the duckling, "so delicious when the waters close over your head, and you plunge to the bottom."

"Well, that is a queer sort of pleasure," said the hen; "I think you must be crazy. Not to speak of myself, ask the cat—he is the wisest creature I know—whether he would like to swim, or to plunge to the bottom of the water. Ask your mistress: no one is cleverer than she. Do you think she would take pleasure in swimming, and in the waters closing over her head?"

"You do not understand me," said the duckling.

"What! we do not understand you! So you think yourself wiser than the cat and the old woman, not to speak of myself! Do not fancy any such thing, child, but be thankful for all the kindness that has been shown you. Are you not lodged in a warm room, and have you not the advantage of society from which you can learn something? But you are a chatterbox and it is wearisome to listen to you. Believe me, I wish you well. I tell you unpleasant truths, but it is thus that real friendship is shown. Come, for once give yourself the trouble either to learn to purr, or to lay eggs."

"I think I will take my chance and go out into the wide world again," said the duckling.

"Well, go then," said the hen.

So the duckling went away. He soon found water and swam on the surface and plunged beneath it, but all other animals passed him by, because of his ugliness. The autumn came: the leaves turned yellow and brown, the wind caught them and danced about, the air was very cold, the clouds were heavy with hail or snow, and the raven sat on the hedge and croaked. The poor duckling was certainly not very comfortable!

One evening, just as the sun was setting, a flock of large birds rose from the brushwood. The duckling had never seen anything so beautiful before; their plumage was of dazzling white, and they had long, slender necks. They were swans. They uttered a singular cry, spread out their long, splendid wings, and flew away from these cold regions to warmer countries, across the sea. They flew so high, so very high! and the ugly duckling's feelings were very strange. He turned round and round in the water like a wheel, strained his neck to look after them, and sent forth such a loud and strange cry, that it almost frightened him. Ah! he could not forget them, those noble birds, those happy birds! The duckling knew not what the birds were called, knew not whither they were flying, yet he loved them as he had never before loved anything. He envied them not. It would never have occurred to him to wish such beauty for himself. He would have been quite contented if the ducks in the duck yard had but endured his company.

And the winter was cold, so cold! The duckling had to swim round and round in the water to keep from freezing. But every

night the opening in which he swam became smaller and smaller; the duckling had to make good use of his legs to prevent the water from freezing entirely. At last, wearied out, he lay stiff and cold in the ice.

Early in the morning there passed by a peasant, who saw him, broke the ice in pieces with his wooden shoes, and carried the duckling home to his wife.

The duckling soon revived. The children would have played with him, but he thought they wished to tease him and in his terror jumped into the milk pail, so that the milk was splashed about the room. The good woman screamed and clapped her hands. He flew first into the tub where the butter was kept, and then into the meal barrel, and out again.

The woman screamed and struck at him with the tongs; the children ran races with each other trying to catch him, and laughed and screamed likewise. It was well for him that the door stood open; he jumped out among the bushes into the newly-fallen snow, and lay there as in a dream.

But it would be too sad to relate all the trouble and misery he had to suffer during the winter. He was lying on a moor among the reeds when the sun began to shine warmly again. The larks were singing, and beautiful spring had returned.

Once more he shook his wings. They were stronger than before and bore him forward quickly; and before he was well aware of it, he was in a large garden where the apple trees stood in full bloom, where the elder trees sent forth their fragrance and hung their long green branches down into the winding canal. Oh! everything was so lovely, so full of the freshness of spring!

Out of the thicket came three beautiful white swans. They displayed their feathers so proudly, and swam lightly, so lightly! The duckling knew the glorious creatures and was seized with a strange sadness.

"I will fly to them, those kindly birds!" said he. "They will kill me, because I, ugly as I am, have presumed to approach them. But it matters not. Better be killed by them than be bitten by the ducks, pecked by the hens, kicked by the girl who feeds the poultry, and have so much to suffer during the winter!" He flew into the water and swam towards the beautiful creatures. They saw him and shot forward to meet him. "Kill me," said the poor duckling, and he bowed his head low, expecting death. But what did he see in the water? He saw beneath him his own form, no longer that of a plump, ugly gray bird—it was that of a swan!

It matters not if one is born in a duck yard, if one has been hatched from a swan's egg.

The larger swans swam round him and stroked him with their beaks, and he was very happy.

Some little children were running about in the garden. They threw grain and bread into the water, and the youngest exclaimed, "There is a new one!" The others also cried out, "Yes, a new swan has come!" and they clapped their hands and ran and told their father and mother. Bread and cake were thrown into the water, and everyone said, "The new one is the best, so young and handsome, and so beautiful!" and the old swans bowed before him.

The young swan felt quite ashamed, and hid his head under his wing. He was all too happy, but still not proud, for a good heart is never proud.

He remembered how he had been laughed at and cruelly treated, and he now heard everyone say he was the most beautiful of all beautiful birds.

The elder trees bent down their branches towards him, and the sun shone warmly and brightly. He shook his feathers, stretched his slender neck, and in the joy of his heart said, "How little did I dream of so much happiness when I was the ugly, despised duckling!"

The Little Tin Soldier

There were once five-and-twenty tin soldiers, all brothers, for all had been made out of one old tin spoon. They carried muskets in their arms and held themselves very upright, and their uniforms were red and blue. The first words they heard in this world were, "Tin soldiers!" It was a little boy who uttered them, when the lid was taken off the box where they lay; and he clapped his hands with delight. They had been given to him because it was his birthday. Then he set them out on the table.

The soldiers were like each other to a hair; all but one, who had only one leg, because he had been made last, when there was not quite enough tin left. He stood as firmly, however, upon his one leg as the others did upon their two, and it is this one-legged tin soldier's fortunes that seem to us worthy of being told.

On the table where the tin soldiers stood there were other play-things, but the most charming of them all was a pretty pasteboard castle. Through its little windows one could look into the rooms. In front of the castle stood some tiny trees, clustering round a little mirror intended to represent a lake. Some waxen swans swam on the lake and were reflected in it.

All this was very pretty, but prettiest of all was a little lady standing in front of the castle. She, too, was cut out of pasteboard, but she had on a beautiful frock of the softest muslin, and she wore a glittering tinsel rose. The little lady was a dancer, and she stretched out both her arms, and raised one of her legs so high in the air that the tin soldier could not see it, and thought she had, like himself, only one leg.

"That would be just the wife for me," thought he, "but then she is of too high a rank. She lives in a castle, and I have only a

box, and even that is not my own, for all our five-and-twenty men live in it; so it is no place for her. Still, I must make her acquaintance." Then he laid himself down at full length behind a snuffbox that stood on the table so that he had a full view of the delicate little lady still standing on one leg without losing her balance.

When evening came, all the other tin soldiers were put into the box, and the people of the house went to bed. Then the playthings began to play games, to pay visits, fight battles and to give balls. The tin soldiers rattled in the box, for they wished to play too, but the lid would not open. The nutcrackers pranced about, and the slate pencil danced about on the table. There was such a noise that the canary woke up and began to talk too, but he always talked in verse. The only two who did not move from their places were the tin soldier and the dancer. She remained standing on the very tip of her toes, with outstretched arms, and he stood just

as firmly on his one leg, never for a moment taking his eyes off her.

Twelve o'clock struck, and with a crash the lid of the snuff-box sprang open—there was no snuff in it, it was only a toy puzzle—and out jumped a little black wizard. "Tin soldier!" said the wizard, "please keep your eyes to yourself!"

But the tin soldier pretended not to hear.

"Well, just wait till tomorrow!" said the wizard.

When the children got up next morning the tin soldier was placed on the window ledge, and, whether the wizard or the wind caused it, all at once the window flew open and out fell the tin soldier head foremost, from the third story to the ground.

It was a dreadful fall, for he fell headfirst into the street, and at last rested with his cap and bayonet between two paving stones, and with his one leg in the air.

The maidservant and the little boy came downstairs directly to look for him; but though they very nearly trod on him they could not see him. If the tin soldier had but called out, "Here I am!" they might easily have found him, but he thought it would not be becoming for him to cry out, as he was in uniform.

Presently it began to rain; soon the drops were falling thicker, and there was a perfect downpour. When it was over, two little children came by.

"Look," said one, "there is a tin soldier. Let him have a sail for once in his life."

So they made a boat out of newspaper, and put the soldier into it. Away he sailed down the gutter, both the boys running along by the side of it and clapping their hands. The paper boat rocked to and fro, and every now and then was whirled round so quickly that the tin soldier became quite giddy. Still he did not move a muscle but looked straight before him, and held his musket tightly clasped.

All at once the boat was carried into a long drain, where the tin soldier found it as dark as in his own box.

"Where can I be going now?" thought he. "It is all that wizard's doing. Ah! if only the little maiden were sailing with me I would not mind its being twice as dark."

Just then a great water rat that lived in the drain darted out. "Have you a passport?" asked the rat. "Show me your passport!" But the tin soldier was silent, and held his musket tighter than ever. The boat sailed on, and the rat followed. How he gnashed his teeth, and cried out to the sticks and the straws: "Stop him, stop him, he has not paid the toll; he has not even shown his passport." But the stream grew stronger and stronger. The tin

soldier could already catch a glimpse of the daylight where the tunnel ended, but at the same time he heard a roaring noise that might have made the boldest tremble. Where the tunnel ended, the water of the gutter fell into a great canal. This was as dangerous for the tin soldier as a waterfall would be for us.

The fall was now so close that he could no longer stand upright. The boat darted forward; the poor tin soldier held himself as stiffly as possible, so that no one could accuse him of having even blinked. The boat spun round three or four times, and was filled with water to the brim; it began to sink.

The tin soldier stood up to his neck in water, but deeper and deeper sank the boat, and softer and softer grew the paper till the water stood over the soldier's head. He thought of the pretty little dancer whom he would never see again, and these words rang in his ears:

"Fare on, thou soldier brave!
Life must end in the grave."

The paper now split in two, and the tin soldier fell through and was at once swallowed up by a large fish. Oh, how dark it was! darker even than in the tunnel and much narrower too! But the tin soldier was as dauntless as ever and lay there at full length, still shouldering his arms.

The fish swam to and fro and made the strangest movements, but at last he became quite still. After a while a flash of lightning seemed to dart through him and the daylight shone brightly, and someone cried out, "I declare, here is the tin soldier!" The fish had been caught, taken to the market, sold, and brought into the kitchen, where the cook was cutting him up with a large knife. She seized the tin soldier by the middle with two fingers, and took him into the parlor, where everyone was eager to see

the wonderful man who had traveled in the stomach of a fish. But the tin soldier was not proud.

They set him on the table, and—what strange things do happen in the world!—the tin soldier was in the very room in which he had been before. He saw the same children, the same playthings on the table—among them the beautiful castle with the pretty little dancing maiden, who was still standing upon one leg while

she held the other high in the air; she too was unbending. It quite touched the tin soldier; he could have found it in his heart to weep tin tears, but such weakness would have been unbecoming in a soldier. He looked at her and she looked at him, but neither spoke a word.

And now one of the boys took the soldier and threw him into the stove. He gave no reason for doing so, but no doubt it was the fault of the wizard in the snuffbox.

The tin soldier now stood in a blaze of light. He felt extremely hot, but whether from the fire or from the flames of love he did not know. He had entirely lost his color. Whether this was the result of his travels, or the effect of strong feeling, I know not. He looked at the little lady, and she looked at him, and he felt that he was melting, but, erect as ever, he still stood shouldering

his arms. Suddenly a door opened, and the draft caught the dancer, and, like a sylph, she flew straightway into the stove, to the tin soldier. Instantly she was in a blaze and was gone. The soldier was melted and dripped down among the ashes, and when

the maid cleaned out the fireplace the next day she found his
remains in the shape of a little tin heart. Of the dancer all that
was left was the tinsel rose, and that was burned as black as coal.

Thumbelina

Once upon a time there was a woman who wished very much for a little child, but did not know where to find one. So at last she went to a witch and said to her: "I do so much wish to have a little child; can you, who are so wise, tell me where I can find one?"

"I can easily do so," said the witch. "There is nothing easier. Here is a barleycorn, but it is quite unlike those that grow in the farmers' fields and that the fowls eat. Put it into a flowerpot and wait and see what takes place."

"Oh, thank you so much," said the woman, giving the witch twelve pennies, which was the price she asked for her barley-corn. Thereafter she went straight home and planted the barley-corn, and at once a large handsome flower sprang up. It looked something like a tulip, but its leaves were tightly closed, as if they were the leaves of a bud. "What a lovely flower!" said the woman, kissing its red and golden-colored leaves. At her kiss the leaves burst open with a crack and she saw that it was really a tulip such as one can see almost anywhere. But lo! in the very center of the blossom, on one of the velvety stamens, sat a tiny maiden, a delicate and graceful little creature, scarcely half as long as a thumb, and when the woman saw her she called her Thumbelina, because she was so small.

A finely polished walnut shell formed her cradle, and therein, on a bed of violets, under a rose-leaf coverlet, Thumbelina slept soundly at night. During the day she amused herself by floating across a plate full of water in a large tulip leaf which served her for a boat. The woman had placed the plate of water on a table and put a wreath of flowers round the edge of it, and from side to side of the plate the little maiden rowed herself with two oars made of white horsehair. It was pretty to see her and prettier still to hear her singing in a voice as clear as a tiny silver bell. Such singing had certainly never been heard before.

One night as she lay asleep in her pretty little bed, a large ugly old toad crept through a broken pane in the window and leaped upon the table. "What a lovely little creature this is!" she thought. "And what a charming wife she would make for my son!" So she took up the walnut shell in which the little maiden lay asleep under her coverlet of rose leaf, and leaped with it through the window, and hopped back again into the garden.

Now through the garden a broad stream flowed, and in its marshy banks the old toad lived with her son. He was uglier even than his mother, and when he saw the pretty little maiden in her beautiful bed he was able only to cry in his harsh voice, "Croak, croak, croak."

"Don't make such noise," said the old toad, "or you will wake her and then she may fly away, for she is as light as thistledown. We will put her on one of the large water lily leaves that grow in the middle of the stream. It will seem an island to her, she is so small. She will not be able to get away from it, and we shall have plenty of time to get ready the stateroom under the marsh, where you are to live when you are married."

Out in the middle of the stream grew a number of water lilies, with broad green leaves that floated on top of the water. The largest of these leaves seemed much farther off than any of the rest, and thither the old toad swam, carrying with her the walnut shell in which Thumbelina still lay sound asleep.

Very early in the morning the poor little creature awoke, and when she saw where she was she began to cry bitterly, for water surrounded the leaf on all sides, and she could see no way of ever reaching the land.

Meanwhile, down in the marsh the old toad was as busy as possible decking out her room with sedge and yellow rushes, so as to make it pretty and comfortable for her new daughter-in-law. When she had finished her work she swam out with her ugly son to the leaf where she had placed poor Thumbelina. She wished to carry off the pretty bed, and put it in the bridal chamber to be ready for the bride. To the little maiden the old toad in the water bowed low and said, "Here is my son. He is to be your husband, and you will have a very happy life together in the fine house I have prepared for you down in the marsh by the stream."

"Croak, croak, croak," was all the ugly son could say for himself.

So the old toad and her son took up the pretty little cradle and swam away with it, leaving Thumbelina sitting weeping all alone on the green lily leaf. She could not bear to think of living all alone with the old toad, and of having her ugly son for a husband.

Now the little fishes, who had been swimming about in the water, and had seen the old toad and had heard every word she said, leaped up till their heads were above the water, so that they might see the little girl; and when they caught sight of her they saw that she was very pretty, and they felt very sorry that any one so pretty should have to go and live with the ugly toads.

"No, no!" said they. "Such a thing must never be allowed."

So all the little fishes gathered together in the water round the green stalk of the leaf on which the little maiden sat, and they bit the stalk with their teeth until at last they bit it through. Then away went the leaf sailing quickly down the stream, and carrying Thumbelina far away where the toad could never reach her.

Past many towns she sailed, and when the birds in the bushes saw her they sang, "What a lovely little girl!" On floated the leaf,

carrying her farther and farther away, until at last she came to
another land. Round her head a pretty little white butterfly kept
fluttering constantly, till at last he settled on the leaf. He was
greatly pleased with Thumbelina, and she was glad of it, for it
was not possible now that the ugly toad could ever reach her, and

the land through which she was sailing was very beautiful, and the sun shone on the water till it glowed and sparkled like silver. Thumbelina tied the butterfly to the leaf, which now sped on much faster than before, having the butterfly for a sail, taking the little maiden with it.

Presently a great beetle flew past. The moment he caught sight of the maiden he seized her, putting his claws round her slim waist, and away he flew with her into a tree. But the green leaf floated on down the river, and the butterfly flew with it, for he was tied to the leaf and could not get away.

Oh, how frightened Thumbelina was when the beetle took her with him into the tree! She was sorry, too, for the pretty white butterfly which she had tied to the leaf, for if he could not free himself, he would certainly die of hunger. But the beetle did not worry himself about that. He sat down beside her on one of the leaves of the tree, and gave her some honey from a flower to eat, and told her that she was very pretty, though not like a beetle. In a little while all the beetles that lived in the tree came to visit her. They stared their hardest at Thumbelina, and one young lady beetle said, "Why, she has only two legs! How ugly that looks!"

"She has no feelers," said another; "how stupid she must be!" "How slender her waist is!" said a third. "Pooh! she looks just like a human being."

"How ugly she is!" said all the lady beetles. Thumbelina was really very lovely, and the beetle who had carried her off thought so; but when they all said she was ugly, he began to think that it must be true. So he would have nothing more to say to Thumbelina, but told her that she might go where she pleased. Then the beetles flew down with her from the tree and placed her on a daisy, and Thumbelina wept because she thought she was so ugly that the beetles would have nothing to say to her. And all the time she was in reality one of the loveliest creatures in the world, and as tender and delicate as a rose leaf.

All the summer through poor Thumbelina lived all alone in the forest. She wove for herself a little bed with blades of grass,

and she hung it up under a clover leaf so that she might be sheltered from the rain. For food she sucked the honey from the flowers, and from the leaves every morning she drank the dew. So the summer and the autumn passed away, and then came the long cold winter. The birds that had sung to her so sweetly had all flown away; the trees had lost their leaves, and the flowers were withered. The great clover leaf under whose shelter she had lived was now rolled together and shriveled up, and nothing of it was left but a yellow withered stalk.

Poor Thumbelina felt very, very cold, for her clothes were torn, and she was such a frail, delicate little thing that she nearly died. The snow, too, began to fall, and each flake, as it fell on her, was like a whole shovelful falling on one of us, for we are tall, and she was only very tiny. Then she rolled herself up in a dry leaf, but it cracked in the middle, and there was no warmth in it, so she shivered with cold. Very near the wood in which she had been living there was a large cornfield, but the corn had been cut long before this, and there was nothing left but the hard, dry

stubble standing up out of the frozen ground. To Thumbelina, it was like struggling through another forest; and, oh, how bitterly cold it was! At last she came to the door of the house of a field mouse, who lived in a hole under the stubble. It was a warm, cozy house, and the mouse was very happy, for she had a whole roomful of corn, besides a kitchen and a fine dining room. Poor little Thumbelina stood before the door of the house, just like a beggar girl, and pleaded for a small bit of barleycorn because she was starving, having had nothing to eat for the last two days.

"Poor little thing!" said the field mouse, who was really a kind-hearted old creature, "come into my warm room and have dinner with me." The mouse was greatly pleased with Thumbelina, so she said, "If you like, you can spend the winter with me; of course you will keep my rooms tidy and tell me stories. I am very fond of hearing stories."

Thumbelina did all the kind old mouse asked her, and in return she was well treated and very comfortable. "We shall have a visitor soon," said the field mouse to Thumbelina one day; "my neighbor pays me a visit once a week. He is much richer than I am; he has fine large rooms and wears a beautiful black velvet fur. If you could get him for a husband you would indeed be well off. He is blind though, poor man, so you must tell him some of your prettiest stories." But Thumbelina knew that the neighbor she had spoken of was only a mole, and she did not mean to trouble herself about him.

The mole, however, came and paid his visit. He was dressed in his black velvet coat.

"He is very learned and very rich," whispered the old field mouse to Thumbelina, "and his house is twenty times larger than mine."

Rich no doubt he was, and learned too, but never having seen the sun or the beautiful flowers, he always spoke disparagingly of them. Thumbelina found that she had to sing to him, so she sang, "Ladybird, ladybird, fly away home," and "As I was going along, long, long," and other pretty songs, and the mole at once fell deeply in love with her because she had such a sweet voice; but, being a prudent man, he said nothing about his feelings.

A short time before this visit, the mole had dug a long underground passage between the two houses, and he gave the field mouse and Thumbelina permission to walk in this passage whenever they pleased. But he told them that there was a dead bird lying in the passage, and he begged them not to be frightened by it. The bird, he said, was perfect, with beak and feathers all complete. It could not have been dead long, and had been buried just where he had made the passage. Then the mole took a phosphorescent piece of rotten wood in his mouth, and it shone like fire in the darkness, and he went before them to light the long dark passage. When they came to where the dead bird lay, the mole pushed his broad nose through the ceiling so as to make a hole.

The daylight fell through the hole and shone on the body of a

dead swallow, lying on its back with its pretty wings closely folded. The poor bird had undoubtedly died of cold. It made the little girl very sad to see it, for she dearly loved little birds. All through the summer they had chirped and sung to please her.

But the unfeeling mole thrust the swallow aside with his crooked legs, and said, "He will sing no more now. What a wretched thing it must be to be born a bird. Thank Heaven, none of my children will ever be birds. Birds can do nothing but cry tweet, tweet! and they always starve to death in the winter."

"Indeed, as a sensible man, you may well say so," cried the field mouse. "What does his chirping and twittering do for a bird when the winter comes? Can his tweet, tweet, appease his hunger, or keep him from being frozen to death? And yet it is thought to be very well bred!"

Thumbelina did not speak, but when the other two turned their backs on the dead bird, she stooped down and smoothed aside the feathers that covered its head, and kissed its closed eyelids.

"Perhaps it was you who sang so sweetly to me in the summer," she said, "and how much pleasure you gave me, you dear pretty bird!"

The mole then stopped up the hole through which the daylight came, and walked home with the ladies. But at night Thumbelina could not sleep; so she got out of bed and wove a fine large rug of soft hay. When she had finished it, she gathered together some soft flower down that she found in the field mouse's sitting room, and she carried the rug and the down to the dead bird. The down was soft and warm like wool, and she put it carefully round him and spread the coverlet over him, that he might lie warm in the cold earth.

"Good-bye! you dear, pretty little bird," said she, "good-bye. Thank you for all the sweet songs you sang in the summer when the trees were green and the sun shone down warmly upon us." Sorrowfully she laid her head on the breast of the bird, but almost at once she raised it in surprise. It seemed as if something inside the bird was going "thump, thump." It was the swallow's heart. The swallow was not really dead but only numbed with the cold, and when the warmth stole over him his life came back.

In autumn all the swallows fly away to warmer lands. But if one of them stays behind too long, the cold freezes it and it falls to the ground as if dead. It lies where it falls and the cold snow covers it.

Thumbelina trembled with fear, for the bird seemed very large in comparison with a little thing like herself. But her pity was stronger than her fear, and being a brave little girl, she covered the poor swallow more thickly with the down, and ran and brought a balsam leaf that she herself used as a coverlet and spread it over the bird's head.

Next night she again stole into the passage to see him. He was still alive, but he was very weak and could only open his eyes to look for a moment at his kind little nurse, who stood over him, holding in her hand a rotten piece of wood, for she had no other light.

"Thank you, pretty little maiden," whispered the sick swallow; "I am so nice and warm now that I shall soon get back my strength and be able to fly about again in the warm sunshine."

"Alas!" said she. "You must wait for some time. It is too cold out of doors just now; it snows and freezes. You must stay in your warm bed, and I will take care of you."

Then she brought him some water in a flower leaf; and when he had drunk it he told her how he had wounded one of his wings

in a thorn bush and was not able to fly as fast as the other swallows; how they flew away without him; and how he fell senseless to the ground. He could not remember any more, and did not know how he came to be where he then lay. All the winter the swallow remained underground, and Thumbelina nursed him with the tenderest care. She did not say a word about the sick swallow to the mole or to the field mouse, for they did not like birds. Soon the spring came. The sun warmed the earth, and the swallow said good-bye to his kind little nurse. She opened the hole in the ceiling which the mole had made. The glorious sunshine poured into the passage, and the swallow begged her to go away with him. She could sit on his back, he said, and she could fly away with him into the green woods. But the little maiden knew that it would vex the old field mouse if she left in that way, so she said, "No, I cannot come."

"Good-bye then, good-bye, you pretty little darling," said the swallow, and away he flew into the sunshine. Thumbelina gazed after him and tears filled her eyes. She dearly loved the pretty swallow, whose life she had saved.

"Joy, joy!" sang the bird as he flew away into the green woods. But poor Thumbelina was very sorrowful. She was not able to get out into the warm sunshine, for the corn which the farmer had

sown in the field over the house of the field mouse had grown up so high that it seemed a lofty and pathless wood to the little maiden.

"Now," said the field mouse to her one day, "you are going to be married, Thumbelina. My neighbor, the mole, has proposed to you. What a piece of luck for a poor girl like you! You must begin at once to get your wedding clothes ready. You must have both woolen and linen, for nothing must be wanting in the wedding outfit of a mole's bride."

Thumbelina had set to work with the spindle, and the field

mouse hired four spiders who had to weave day and night. Every evening the mole came to pay his visit, and he always spoke of the time when the summer would be over. Then, he said, they would be married. Just now the sun was so hot that it burned up the ground and made it as hard as stone. But the little maiden was not at all happy. She thought the mole tiresome and did not like him. In the morning when the sun rose, and in the evening when it set, she used to creep out at the door, and when the wind blew aside the ears of corn so that she could catch a glimpse of the blue sky, she used to think how lovely it was in the light, and long to see her dear swallow once more. But he would probably never come back again, for by this time he had flown far, far away into the green woods. When the autumn came Thumbelina had her wedding outfit quite ready, and the field mouse said to her, "Well, Thumbelina, in a month now you shall be married." But the girl cried, and said she would never marry the tiresome mole.

"Nonsense, nonsense!" said the mouse. "Don't be foolish or I shall bite you with my white teeth. The mole will make you a very handsome husband. The Queen herself does not wear such a fine black velvet coat. He has, besides, a full kitchen and cellar. You ought to be very thankful for your good fortune."

At length the wedding day arrived. The mole came to fetch his bride. Thumbelina would have to go away and live with him deep under the earth, and never again see the warm sun because he did not like it. The poor little maid was very sad at the thought of saying farewell to the beautiful sun, and as the field mouse had permitted her to stand at the door, she went out to look at it once more, and to say farewell to it.

"Farewell, dear bright sun," she cried, stretching out her arms towards it. Then she walked a little way from the house, for the corn had been cut, and there was only the dry stubble left in the fields. "Farewell, farewell!" she said again, throwing her arms round a little red flower that grew close beside her. "Give my love to the swallow, if you should ever see him again."

Suddenly, a "tweet, tweet" sounded over her head. She looked up, and there was the swallow himself flying past. As soon as he spied Thumbelina he flew to her with delight, and she told him her story, told him how unwilling she was to marry the stupid mole, and to live always under the earth, and never again see the bright sun. As she told him about her marriage she could not help weeping.

"The cold winter is coming now," said the swallow, "and I am going to fly away to a warmer land. Will you come with me? You can sit on my back. Tie yourself on with your sash. Then we will fly away from the ugly mole and his gloomy abode, fly far away over the hills to warmer lands—lands where the sunshine is brighter than it is here, where there are lovely flowers, and where it is always summer. Fly away with me now, dear little Thumbelina. You saved my life when I lay frozen in yonder black tunnel."

"Yes, I will come with you," said the little maiden. Then she sat down on the bird's back with her feet resting on his outspread wings, and she fastened her sash to one of his stronger feathers; and the swallow rose high into the air, and flew fast over forest and lake, and over the snow-capped mountains. Poor Thumbelina would have been frozen but she crept under the bird's warm feathers, peeping out from time to time so that she might catch a glimpse of the beautiful lands over which they were passing. At last they reached the warm countries, where the sun shines much more brightly than it does here, and where the sky seems twice as high above the earth. There by the wayside and on the hedges there grew purple and green and white grapes, and pale lemons and golden oranges hung from the trees in the woods. The air was fragrant with the scent of myrtle and balm, and along the country lanes ran beautiful children, playing with large gay butterflies. The farther the swallow flew the more beautiful every place seemed to grow. At last they came to a lovely blue lake,

and by the side of it, shaded by stately green trees, stood a pure white marble castle. It was an old building, and the vine leaves twined round its lofty columns. At the top of these there were many swallows' nests, and one of these was the nest of the swallow who carried Thumbelina.

"This is my house," said the swallow; "but it would not do for you to live here. Will you choose for yourself one of those beautiful flowers?—and I will put you down on it, and then you shall have everything you can wish to make you happy."

"That will be charming," cried the little maiden, and she clapped her tiny hands.

On the ground lay a large white marble pillar, which had fallen and been broken into three pieces. Between the pieces grew the most beautiful large white flowers. The swallow flew down with Thumbelina and set her on one of the broad leaves. But how surprised she was to see in the middle of the flower a tiny little man as white and transparent as glass! On his head was a graceful

golden crown, and at his shoulders a pair of delicate wings. He was not much larger than the little maid herself. He was the flower elf. An elf man and an elf maid lived in every flower, and he was the King of all the flower elves.

"Oh, how beautiful he is!" whispered Thumbelina to the swallow.

The little flower king was at first quite frightened at the bird. Compared with a little man like himself, it was a giant. But when he saw Thumbelina he was charmed. Never had he seen such a pretty girl. He took the gold crown from his head and placed it on hers; he asked her name, and begged her to marry him, and become the Queen of all the flowers.

This was certainly a very different kind of husband from the son of the toad or from the mole with his black velvet coat, so she said "yes" to this handsome prince, her new suitor. Then all the flowers opened, and out of each came a tiny lady and gentle-man. They were all so graceful that it was a pleasure to look at them. They each brought Thumbelina a present, but the present she loved most of all was a pair of lovely white wings from a big white fly. When these were fastened to her shoulders she could fly from flower to flower.

Then there were great rejoicings, and the little swallow who sat in his nest overhead was asked to sing a wedding song for them. He sang as well as he could, but his heart was sad, for he was very fond of the little maiden and had hoped never again to part from her.

"You must no longer be called Thumbelina," said the flower elf to her. "It's an ugly name, and you are very beautiful. We will call you Maia."

"Good-bye, good-bye," sang the swallow, sad at heart, as he left the warm lands and flew away to the colder North. There he had a nest outside the window of a man who could tell fairy tales. For him the swallow sang "tweet, tweet," and that's how we came to hear the whole story.

The Emperor's New Clothes

Many years ago there was an Emperor who was so very fond of new clothes that he spent all his money on dress. He did not trouble himself in the least about his soldiers, nor did he care to go either to the theater or to hunt, except for the occasion they gave him for showing off his new clothes. He had a different suit for each hour of the day; and as one is accustomed to say of any other king or emperor, "He is sitting in council," it was always said of him, "The Emperor is sitting in his wardrobe."

Time passed merrily in the large town that was his capital. Strangers arrived at the court every day. One day two rogues, calling themselves weavers, made their appearance. They said that they knew how to weave fabrics of the most beautiful colors and patterns, but that the clothes made from these had the wonderful property of remaining invisible to every one who was either stupid or unfit for the office he held.

"Those would indeed be splendid clothes!" thought the Emperor. "Had I such a suit, I might at once find out what men in my realms are unfit for their office, and be able to distinguish the wise from the foolish. This fabric must be woven for me immediately." And he gave large sums of money to the weavers, that they might begin their work at once.

123

So the rogues set up two looms, and made a show of working very busily, though in reality they had nothing at all on the looms. They asked for the finest silk and the purest gold thread, put both into their own knapsacks, and then continued their pretended work at the empty looms until late at night.

"I should like to know how the weavers are getting on with my cloth," thought the Emperor after some time. He was, how-

ever, rather nervous when he remembered that a stupid person, or one unfit for his office, would be unable to see the cloth. "To be sure," he thought, "I have nothing to risk in my own person; but yet I would prefer sending somebody else to bring me news about the weavers and their work, before I trouble myself in the affair." All the city had heard of the wonderful property the cloth was to possess, and all were anxious to learn how worthless and stupid their neighbors were.

"I will send my faithful old minister to the weaver's," concluded the Emperor at last. "He will be best able to see how the cloth looks, for he is a man of sense, and no one can be better fitted for his post than he is."

So the faithful old minister went into the hall where the two swindlers were working with all their might at their empty looms. "What can be the meaning of this?" thought the old man, opening his eyes very wide. "I can't see the least bit of thread on the looms!" However, he did not speak aloud.

The rogues begged him most respectfully to be so good as to come nearer, and then asked whether the design pleased him and whether the colors were not very beautiful, pointing at the same time to the empty frames. The poor old minister looked and looked; he could see nothing on the looms, for there was nothing there. "What!" thought he, "is it possible that I am silly? I have never thought so myself; and no one must know it now. Can it

be that I am unfit for my office? It will never do for me to say that I could not see the cloth."

"Well, Sir Minister!" said one of the rogues, still pretending to work, "you do not say whether the cloth pleases you."

"Oh, it's very fine!" said the old minister, looking at the loom through his spectacles. "The pattern and the colors are wonderful. Yes, I will tell the Emperor without delay how very beautiful I think them."

"We are glad they please you," said the swindlers, and then they named the different colors and described the pattern of the pretended fabric. The old minister paid close attention, that he might repeat to the Emperor what they said.

Then the swindlers asked for more silk and gold, saying it was needed to complete what they had begun. Of course, they put all that was given them into their knapsacks, and kept on as before working busily at their empty looms.

The Emperor now sent another officer of his court to see how the men were getting on, and to find out whether the cloth would soon be ready. It was just the same with him as with the first. He looked and looked, but could see nothing at all but the empty looms.

"Isn't it fine cloth?" asked the rogues. The minister said he thought it beautiful. Then they began as before, pointing out its beauties and talking of patterns and colors that were not there.

"I certainly am not stupid," thought the officer. "It must be that I am not fit for my post. That seems absurd. However, no one shall know it." So he praised the cloth he could not see, and said he was delighted with both colors and patterns. "Indeed, Your Majesty," said he to the Emperor when he gave his report, "the cloth is magnificent."

The whole city was talking of the splendid cloth that the Emperor was having woven at his own cost.

And now the Emperor thought he would like to see the cloth while it was still on the loom. Accompanied by a select number of officials, among whom were the two honest men who had already admired the cloth, he went to the cunning weavers who, when aware of the Emperor's approach, went on working more busily than ever, although they did not pass a single thread through the looms.

"Is it not absolutely magnificent?" said the two officers who had been there before. "If Your Majesty will only be pleased to look at it! what a splendid design! what glorious colors!" And at the same time they pointed to the empty looms, for they thought that everyone else could see the cloth.

"How is this?" said the Emperor to himself; "I can see nothing! Oh, this is dreadful! Am I a fool? Am I unfit to be an Emperor? That would be the worst thing that could happen to me. Oh! the cloth is charming," said he aloud. "It has my complete approval." And he smiled most graciously and looked closely at the empty looms; for on no account would he say he could not see what two of the officers of his court had praised so much. All the people now looked and looked, but they could see nothing more than the others. Nevertheless, they all exclaimed, "Oh, how beautiful!" and advised His Majesty to have some new clothes made from this splendid material for the approaching procession. "Magnificent! charming! excellent!" resounded on all sides; and everyone seemed greatly pleased. The Emperor showed his satisfaction by making the rogues knights, and giving them the title of "Gentlemen Weavers to the Emperor."

The two rogues sat up the whole of the night before the day of the procession. They had sixteen candles burning, so that everyone might see how hard they were working to finish the Emperor's new suit. They pretended to roll the cloth off the looms; they cut the air with great scissors, and sewed with needles without any thread in them. "See!" cried they at last, "the Emperor's new clothes are ready!"

And now the Emperor, with his grandest courtiers, went to the weavers. The rogues raised their arms, as if holding something up, and said, "Here are Your Majesty's trousers! here is the scarf! here is the cloak! The whole suit is as light as a cobweb. You might fancy you had on nothing at all when dressed in it; that, however, is the great virtue of this fine cloth."

"Yes, indeed!" said all the courtiers, although not one of them could see anything, because there was nothing to be seen.

"If Your Imperial Majesty will be graciously pleased to take off your clothes, we will fit on the new suit before the great mirror," said the swindlers.

The Emperor accordingly took off his clothes, and the swindlers pretended to put on him separately each article of his new suit, the Emperor turning round from side to side in front of the mirror.

"How splendid His Majesty looks in his new clothes! and how well they fit!" everyone cried out. "What a design! what colors! These are indeed royal robes!"

"The attendants are waiting outside with the canopy which is to be carried over Your Majesty in the procession," announced the chief master of the ceremonies.

"I am quite ready," answered the Emperor. "Do my new clothes fit well?" he asked, turning himself round again before the mirror as if he were carefully examining his handsome suit.

The lords of the bedchamber, who were to carry His Majesty's train, felt about on the ground, as if they were lifting up the end of the cloak, and walked as if they were holding up a train; for they feared to show that they saw nothing and so be thought stupid or unfit for their office.

So in the midst of the procession the Emperor walked under his high canopy through the streets of his capital. And all the

people standing by, and those at the windows, cried out, "Oh! how beautiful are our Emperor's new clothes! what a train there is to the cloak! and how gracefully the scarf hangs!" In short, no one would admit that he could not see those much admired clothes, because, in doing so, he would have declared himself either a fool or unfit for his office. Certainly, none of the Emperor's previous suits had made such an impression as this.

"But the Emperor has nothing on at all!" said a little child.

"Listen to the voice of innocence!" exclaimed her father; and what the child had said was whispered from one to another.

"But he has nothing on at all!" at last cried out all the people. The Emperor was vexed, for he felt that the people were right; but he thought the procession must go on now. And the lords of the bedchamber took greater pains than ever to appear to be holding up a train, although, in reality, there was no train to hold.